Ariel's Royal Wedding

DISNEY PRESS

New York • Los Angeles

ISBN 978-1-4847-1679-3
F383-2370-2-14146
Printed in China
First Edition
1 3 5 7 9 10 8 6 4 2
For more Disney Press fun, visit www.disneybooks.com

Ariel loved Prince Eric from the moment she first saw him, even though she was a mermaid and he was a human. And Prince Eric loved Ariel from the moment he heard her sing.

Now they were getting married!

Ariel had never been to a human wedding before. She wasn't sure what to do. She found Grimsby busily preparing the guest list. Ariel was puzzled. "Why is the list so long?"

"A wedding is for the family as much as it is for the bride and groom," said Grimsby.

That made Ariel think about her own family. They all lived under the sea. Would they be able to come to her wedding?

Lost in thought, Ariel wandered into town. Before she knew it, she was surrounded by people in the marketplace—all offering items for her wedding.

"Gee, thank you!" Ariel exclaimed. "But I—I'm not sure what I need for a human wedding. Not yet, anyway." Blushing, she ran back to the palace.

Back at the palace, Ariel hesitantly approached Grimsby. In the village she had heard that human couples, like merfolk, danced at weddings.

"I don't know how to dance—at least not with legs," she admitted shyly.

"One, two, three, one, two, three," Grimsby said as he instructed Ariel in a waltz.

Before long, she was twirling like an expert across the floor.

Ariel knew Carlotta would be the best person to ask about a wedding dress. "What does a human wedding dress feel like? Is it hard to walk in?"

"A human wedding dress has to be beautiful and billowy and white!" Carlotta said, excitedly sketching one dress idea after another. "It has to be made of the finest silks and satins! I promise you will have no problem walking in it."

With the help of Carlotta, the royal dressmaker worked through the night, sewing Ariel's dream dress. "It's so beautiful!" cried Ariel.

The next morning, Ariel visited Chef Louis in the kitchen. He was busy preparing the wedding menu and baking sample wedding cakes.

"Chef Louis, I don't know what a proper human wedding cake is like," Ariel admitted.

"Don't worry, madam," he said, showing her a sketch. "I will bake you the most delicious, most exquisite wedding cake in all the land and sea!"

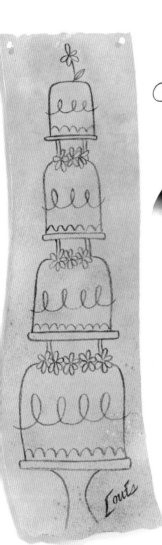

"It's lovely!" cried Ariel. "But it still feels like something is missing. I wish my family could see it."

As Ariel thought about all of the wonderful wedding plans, she began to think about what Grimsby had told her: a wedding is for family.

It was Ariel's dream to spend the rest of her life as Eric's wife, but she wanted her family close by on her wedding day. She began to feel sad.

Later, Eric found Ariel alone on the balcony. He noticed tears in Ariel's eyes. "What's the matter?" he asked.

"I want a human wedding, but I just wish—I just wish that my family could be could be there, too."

"Hmm, I thought you might want that. It's all planned—we'll be married on the royal ship at sea."

"That's perfect!" she cried. "I'll tell them right away."

So Ariel went to see her family. She asked her sisters to
be her bridesmaids. She asked Sebastian to be the ring bearer.
And she asked her father, King Triton, to give her away.

"It would be an honor," he said.

Ariel's family helped her find something old, new, borrowed, and blue.

"You can borrow my favorite seashell hair clip," said her sister Aquata.

King Triton took Ariel's hand and gently placed a pink pearl inside of it. It glistened like the shining sea. "This belonged to your mother," he said. "She would've wanted you to have it."

"And you can have my blue starfish," said her sister Adella. "It always brings me good luck."

Ariel hugged her father and thanked her sisters for their help. "I'll see you on my wedding day!" she said to them with happiness in her heart.

Finally, the day of the wedding arrived.
The human guests were all seated on the
deck. The merfolk looked on from the sea.
Ariel's father used the magic of his
trident to lift him and her sisters up to the
side of the ship.

The vows were read. The rings were exchanged.
"Go ahead! Kiss the girl!" cried Sebastian.
And at last, the prince and princess were married!

Next came the cake. The merfolk were surprised when Chef Louis personally sent them a delicious cake to sample as Eric and Ariel shared their first bite of wedding cake.

Sebastian led the sea animal orchestra.
On the deck, Eric and Ariel danced together
for the first time as husband and wife.

Eric and Ariel's wedding day was a celebration for both land and sea—the beginning of a life filled with joy and laughter shared with family and friends of all kinds.